D0629897

For Meg, Sam, and Chris – F. T.

Flying Frog Publishing

© 2008 Flying Frog Publishing
Imprint of Allied Publishing Group, Inc.
Baltimore, MD 21136
Printed in China

Dear Tooth Fairy

The True Story of How the Tooth Fairy Came to Be

Written by Kath Mellentin & Tim Wood

Illustrated by Fran Thatcher

As you know, fairies watch over the Land of Humans and take care of the children who live there. But many years ago something went terribly wrong. The sound of children's laughter floating across Fairy Land stopped. Instead, the fairies could hear only sobbing.

The Fairy Queen sent messengers to find out what was wrong. When they returned, she called a meeting in the Bluebell Woods.

One by one the messengers reported what they had discovered.

"I couldn't find a single reason for all the tears," announced the Laughter Fairy. "I believe the children are sad because they are bored."

"But that can't be true," retorted the Fun Fairy. "Only last week I invented a hundred new games! I think the children are tired."

"Oh no," murmured the Sleep Fairy dreamily. "I cast such beautiful dream spells during my travels that now all the children sleep deeply through the night. I think they're miserable because there's a shortage of delicious things to eat."

"The children have never eaten so many scrumptious cakes and sweets." protested the Treat Fairy.

"Well," interrupted the Queen impatiently, "what is the matter with them?"

The fairies wrinkled their brows and fluttered their wings in puzzlement.

Suddenly there was a small cough. A very nervous young sprite stepped forward.

"Speak up clearly, my dear," said the Queen kindly.

"I think the children are crying because they have too many delicious foods to eat," the sprite began bravely. "Everyone knows that cakes and candies taste good, but too many can cause toothaches."

Gasps of horror rippled among the fairies.

"She could be right!" exclaimed the Treat Fairy. "I did notice that some of my most special sweets were being left uneaten. Nobody can resist a double-decker triple-ripple dreamy-creamy chocolate-coated toffee cake... unless something is wrong."

The fairies all nodded in agreement.

The Queen raised her wand for silence.

"If this is true, we must take immediate action," she announced. The Queen then turned to the sprite. "Do you have a plan?" she asked.

The sprite spoke up boldly. "I think we should help the children take care of their teeth."

"Children must be made to look after their teeth," snapped the Rules Fairy. "After all, they only have one set of—"

"The may be true at the moment," interrupted the sprite in excitement. "But we can create a magic spell that gives every child two sets of teeth. Children can practice on the first set of baby teeth. Then when they've learned how to take care of them, they'll grow a second set that are bigger and stronger. These will be their grown-up teeth."

"But what will happen to the baby teeth when they fall out?" asked the Neat and Tidy Fairy, who always wanted to keep things clean.

"We could give children special purses!" squeaked the sprite gleefully. "Then when their baby teeth fall out, children can put the teeth into the purses and place them under their pillows. With a little bit of magic, we'll make the teeth disappear and in their places leave gifts. Some of our magic can be used to help the new teeth grow stong and healthy."

"Bravo!" said the Queen, delighted with the plan. "You shall become the Tooth Fairy! Your job will be to help children look after their teeth!"

The sprite blushed as red as a rose hip at the unexpected honor. At last she would become a real fairy. All she needed now was some help to mix her spell.

That night, under the pale moonlight, the fairies gathered for the spell-making ceremony. They held hands as they stood in a circle around the cauldron. One by one they fluttered forward to add their magic sparkles to the cauldron. The mixture fizzed and bubbled with each new gift.

"I give a lovely white smile," beamed the Laughter Fairy.

"My gift is a minty tingle that makes toothpaste taste nice." twinkled the Fun Fairy, dancing around the cauldron and twirling her wand.

The spell grew until it was the Tooth Fairy's turn to add the final ingredient. She stepped forward and dipped her new wand into the cauldron.

"My touch of magic will stop the hurting when a tooth falls out," she said.

A sparkling cloud of fairy dust swirled around the cauldron. The spell was ready!

The Tooth Fairy then unfurled her shimmering wings. *Waving* to her friends, she fluttered gently up into the night sky and sprinkled tooth magic onto moonbeams.

From that day on children in every corner of the world have had two sets of teeth—first baby teeth to practice on and then a set of strong grown-up teeth. As for the Tooth Fairy, she is busy every night flitting from pillow to pillow, collecting baby teeth and leaving a little bit of magic that helps keep new teeth strong and healthy.

Tooth Diary

Ask a grown-up member of your family how old you were when your first tooth grew in. You were probably about six months old. Kids typically grow twenty baby teeth—also called milk teeth. Eventually these are pushed out by thirty-two new, stronger teeth. If you look after them, they will last you for the rest of your life.

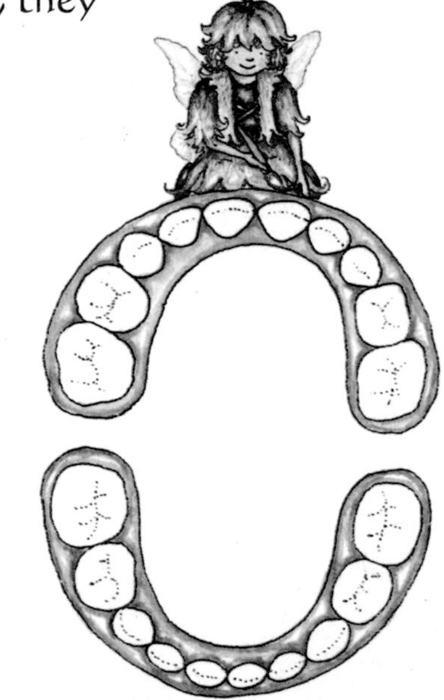

My first baby tooth grew in when I was __________

My first baby tooth fell out when I was __________

My first grown-up tooth grew in when I was ______

As each baby tooth falls out, color it in on this chart.

Tooth Facts

1. Tooth enamel, which protects your teeth, is the hardest part of your whole body!
2. You have baby teeth in your jaw before you are born, but they don't break through the gums until you are about six months old.
3. Buy the time you are six years old, you will have your first grown-up back tooth, even if you can't see it. It sits behind your baby teeth ready to push through.

As each new grown-up tooth grows in, color it in on this chart.

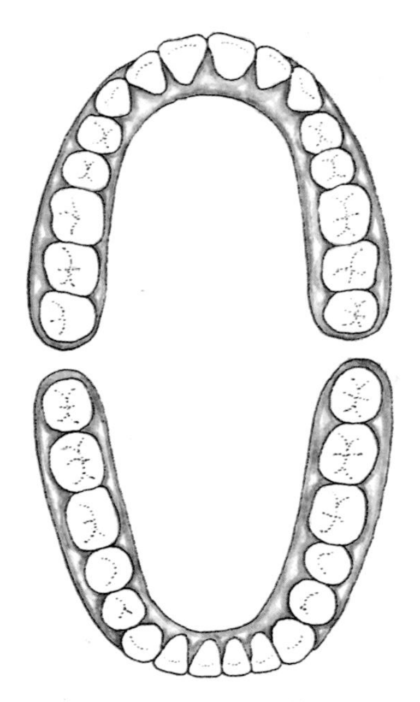

And Remember...

Eat sugary foods, drinks, and sweets only occasionally.

Do not snack between meals. If you want something sweet, eat it with or just after a meal.

Take care to brush your teeth twice a day with a fluoride toothpaste.

Visit your dentist regularly.

Dear "Me"

Milk teeth fall out, but new ones grow
To last you till you're old, and so
Squeeze out a blob of minty paste,
Brush up and down—you'll love the taste.
(If you do this both morn and night
Your smile will stay forever white.)
And see your dentist twice a year,
There really is no need to fear!
The friendly dentist's fun, not scary.

with lots of love from
The Tooth Fairy